I0730953

Requests for permission should be directed to 1111@1111press.com, or mailed to 11:11 Press LLC, 4732 13th Ave S, Minneapolis, MN 55407.

Design by Mike Corrao

Paperback: ISBN

Printed in the United States of America

FIRST AMERICAN EDITION

9 8 7 6 5 4 3 2 1

ALIEN

ALI RAZ

for tvtn

ISSUE ONE:
BEGINNINGS

It happened at night. I was walking home; a stack of bricks hit me in the chest, passed through my skin and slithered through me, into my guts, into my blood. I choked and spluttered, pressed myself against a wall, tried to cough up the thing that had passed into me. Nothing. As suddenly as it had started, the episode came to an end. I was looking at the city street, cars flashing by, taillights blinking in the smog. People passed me on the sidewalk. I could smell a nearby eucalyptus tree, drops of rain still dripping from its leaves.

The man who sold sugarcane juice had left his stall unattended. I paused, then joined the crowd gathered around the juice cart, and when it was my turn I too stole a metal tumbler, filled it with sweet juice, and walked away. I was tired and my feet hurt from a night of searching. As always, I hadn't found anything.

I woke because of the heat. It was blackout time and the generator had stopped working. I lay in bed, stewing in my sweat. The air was thick with the smell of me. When I couldn't bear it any longer, I went up to the roof where I keep the generator. It was noon. There was no wind. I held my breath and crouched by the generator. The plastic casing was hot. I was careful. I poured in more fuel, screwed the cap back on, waited a few seconds, then tugged the rope. With a roar the machine kicked into life, and electricity flooded through my house again.

I went back to bed.

Circadian City. City of *Dreadful Night*

Don't get me wrong. I'm hunting for aliens.

All day I lie on my mattress and listen to the **poet's radio**. It's run by my former friends, the friends I had before I ended them. It's whispers and secret static, for anyone without the code, this station is gibberish. It's transmitted from the hills. You have to know what to listen for. It's all there—everything, the only thing. I keep a journal on my night table and when it comes, as it comes to me, I make sure to inscribe it all. In mirrored handwriting, and under an additional layer of code.

All night I look for aliens.

The aliens are small, humanoid, and blue. They might be mistaken for emaciated infants, were it not for the blue skin and the stumpy pair of hornlike things that sprout from the crown of the head. Antennae. The belly button is thick and protruding. The eyes are large ovals.

Cinema with a friend, FF. She's vivacious, brimming with life. We hold hands in the cool, dark cinema, bathed in the glow of the screen. It's *King Kong*. I imagine we're on a date. I caress her thumb and imagine other things. Something moistens in me.

These memories won't let me sleep. I keep seeing *her face*: pulp. I pace my bedroom all afternoon, remembering her, an ordinary friend, trying to forget her, she is dead and at peace.

Infinite openness and *infinite* malleability. My teeth turn to metal. I laugh with sparkling, metal teeth. *Like a villain, like a villain,* the infinite refrain seethes in me. I roll my eyes back in their sockets, look at my brain. I wake up shivering in sweat. I sit up on my mattress, make a note in my notebook.

A cockroach beats me to the kitchen. I've woken in the night for a glass of water, but when I enter the kitchen there's a cockroach there already, sitting in the middle of the floor, the geometric center. Antennae rubbing. It's thick, black, and silent, sitting in the center of the kitchen. I look at the cockroach. The cockroach looks at me. I make my approach softly, slowly. Then I'm there. Close to the thing. I lift my right foot and bring it down on top of the cockroach. Cracking exoskeleton. Oozing innards. From the counter I grab some tissue paper and wipe the cockroach off my foot. Then I fill a glass with water from the fridge and take it back with me.

Cockroach City

Today I am doing a nearby neighborhood. One I've been to before—but my intuition is buzzing, and I always listen to my intuition. District G. The houses are all the same—small, brown, with tall white gates. I prowl the sidewalks attentively. Tonight's a cool night. Traffic's mild. No one disturbs me. In the distance, a piercing whistle. Then a train. My ears are sharp and I am on high alert, but nothing I notice is out of the ordinary. This worries me.

Ordinary. Nothing here is ordinary.
Ordinary. Nothing here is ordinary.

poet's radio is broadcasting from the hills tonight. I can hear the staticky whisper of a mountain night. It sounds like shiny silver. Tonight I'm restive, want to fight. I fall asleep smiling.

Pack of cheap cigarettes from a tobacco stand. I smoke it right there, slouched in the shade of a banyan tree. The tree whispers secrets to my skin. It's a pleasant itch. I sit under the banyan tree, smoking and drinking tea, and listening to the chatter of the other customers. I absorb all the news, I listen closely. This is how I learn of New Events. No one notices me.

The banyan tree weeps things to me. Its voice is glazed and husky.

I prowl the sidewalks, listening attentively. Voices murmur and swarm in the black air, like the bodies of bees. I must collect this bitter honey. My feet hurt and my legs, from another night of searching, are still sore. I've been losing weight like I'm ill (which I am). It's a hot night. Sweat pours from me. I'm patient; I keep walking. The Map beeps and blinks in me. They leave a trail of traces—disturbances in the air, foreign scents, new textures of anxiety and fear—which I detect with the surface of my skin. I collect these million fragments inside me. Patiently. Patiently. Building something, I don't know what. What dark god gifted me this painful patience?

I was born with asthma and eczema.

A child's corpse in the gutter outside my house. I wake to the rotting smell of it, think they're slaughtering a goat. But when I put on a shirt and go outside, I see a small body crumpled in the gutter, causing an overflow. Filthy water on the street. The size of the corpse sends a thrill through me, but instantly I know I'm mistaken. I crouch. Flip her over with my shoe. She's not older than three. Face snipped with a knife or scissors—incisions all over the cheeks, chin and forehead, flaps of skin hanging from her face, missing the nose. Just a jagged hole where her nose used to be. She's wearing a tattered pink shirt, skirt and sneakers. She's bald. Her eyes are still open, and attracting flies. I flick away a fly, then I call an ambulance I know won't arrive. I go back inside, back to bed, as a crowd begins to form around the body. A high-pitched shriek.

With Q in the old café. It's just the three of us. The owner asleep behind the counter, Q, and me. She asked me why I looked the way I did: pale, underslept, ill. I tried to laugh it off but she wouldn't let me. Finally I lied: I said I was ill with something, *probably nothing, just food poisoning.* We're drinking tea, eating sandwiches, and smoking cigarettes. I keep looking at Q's fingernails, chipped red nail polish. She smells like something. Like rosewater mixed with gasoline.

We ordered chicken sandwiches, but in place of chicken, they're serving dog meat.

Exiting the café, someone attacks us with a tire iron. The iron cracks against my skull. I can taste my blood. I rip off the man's mask and burn his face into my mind. Q's injured, bleeding from the mouth. The man, mask tattered, swaggers off. The owner of the café peeks around the door, solicitous and scared. We wave him away.

I offer to walk Q home, but she refuses. It's only just a surface wound—she pushes my hand away impatiently.

The afternoon passes in blackout.

The wind. This wind. We hide from it.

I play Ludo with neighbors, in my airconditioned room.

They're here for the airconditioning, I know.

From time to time, I send someone to check on the generator. Top off the fuel.

I pluck his coordinates from the air. Pixelated, then clear. I extract his exact coordinates. I follow his cells in the streets, in the wind. His face. Follow the sidewalk cracks in which he's been shedding himself.

He's at home. Eating soup with his grandmother. I push her face into her soup bowl. He rises from his seat, panic flooding him. His muscles start to scream. I remove his teeth with my fingers. Break his bones. Slice his cheeks in a glasgow smile. Hang him upside down from the ceiling fan, set his hair on fire. Watch him burn.

ISSUE TWO:
THE FIRST ALIEN

When I found my first alien, I didn't know what to do with it. I had followed a news report from the tea stall. Someone has spotted a UFO. The man was thin, bearded and raving. He described the UFO as cigar-shaped and hovering in the sky above the roof of his house. He had been sleeping on the roof; the presence of the UFO had penetrated all the way into his dreams, and he described to us the shock of opening his eyes and continuing to see what he had been seeing in his dream.

A metal cigar, hanging in the air.

They have been spotting blue bodies all over the city. These sightings are lost in the other news: dog meat, clouds of white phosphorus, the return of the killer smog.

Return of the killer smog!

It's a film about the smog that covers everything in this city. It's all lies. Everyone knows what this smog is, even if they don't know. The body is never wrong.

That is the film I was watching, on the night I found my first alien. Me and Q, in my living room. My intestines had begun to buzz. I excused myself to the toilet, then found myself climbing out the toilet window. Barefoot, I rushed down nameless dark streets.

It was sitting in a gutter outside District Z. Smaller even than I had expected. I sat down next to it. It had been injured; green fluid puddled around its small, hooved feet. The thing gave off a strange luster, a hot glow that emanated from something inside it. Like an organ of light. We sat in companionable, unstressed silence for several long minutes; then my vision started to blur and distort, gently at first and then it accelerated, until everything around me shrunk into the eye of a needle, became a thin black hole.

That street was demolished the very next day. And all of District Z. Its residents cluttered the roads outside the electric metal fences, wailing every time a wrecking ball tore through a home.

A lizard on my bed. I flinch.

They seep into my room through the walls. I'm masturbating on my bed, and a lizard's eye looks at me from a high corner, snapping photos, logging this image of me inside itself.

I dream of my mother. In this dream, my mother is waiting at a bus stop after school. The summer air fluoresces with heat. My mother is wearing her school uniform: a long, white cotton shirt and loose white pants. Her backpack leans against her leg. My mother, sixteen, waits at the bus stop for a bus that won't come, innocent and smiling, unaware of everything that has gone wrong.

Q holds a gathering of cards, food, and illegal liquor. I enjoy all three. I enjoy the company. My friend's house is large and cozy, proximal to the old part of town. It shares some of the ancient luster of that place, the pride of upright spines. We sit on the carpet in her living room, ten of us, playing cards and talking drunkenly. Someone starts to dance. I watch her lazy, swaying body.

I remember FF again, she who was taken from me. She was taken from herself. One night I walked into my room and found her there, *dead on my bed*, her gullet smashed in several places, vomit and blood in pools on the sheet, her face and chest, and on the floor. Her body had been posed, like for a photo. Facedown, legs spread at 70 degrees, arms flung outwards at right angles, hands dangling over the edge of the bed. And a lizard, pinned above her butt cheeks.

The old part of the city has burned many times. It's impossible to forget this, sitting in Q's living room. Music on her radio. Drops of blood drip from the ceiling, ooze from the walls. I step into blood puddles constantly. Chugging moonshine, I try to knock the awareness from me.

The lizard had been pinned to her shirt with a thin nail, the nail passing through its thick green body and her buttocks, holding it there. It twitched when I touched it.

The music crescendos. Opera. Aria. Someone lets out an exultant whoop. He's holding all the cards. He's won. I look at my hand—

On her face a glasgow smile.

Q moves to sit next to me. She asks me if I like the party. I tell her yes, very much. Thanks for inviting me. She rests her head against my shoulder. Her happiness is a warm wave.

Later, I stay behind to help her clean. We stack the dishes in the sink, pick up litter, straighten the furniture. When we're done we have a cup of tea. We drink it on the roof, under the stars. My friend's tea is warm and sweet. She's exhausted after the party. We talk in low tones, content in our respective positions, like pawns on a chessboard that won't be used.

Walking home, a hand on my shoulder. It makes me startle. A woman's throaty laugh. She comes into sight as a streetlight splutters, CoP. She's a connoisseur of pain. She likes the flogger, whip, and breaking wheel. She's my friend. We walk home hand in hand.

She's brought a jar of moonshine, tucked inside her bra. CoP can hide anything inside her bra. We sit on the sofa in my living room and drink her mango moonshine.

This stuff will make you blind, I tell her, the moonshine eating my throat. She scoffs at me, winks with her clouded green eye.

Then we continue my inculcation into the cult of pain. CoP is my teacher. She makes me do these things. I keep ramming myself inside her as she instructs me, following her orders, her body bored beneath mine. Sometimes I think she's humming a tune. I want to tear through her, make her body yield to mine.

A lizard looks at me upside down, hanging on the ceiling. I see my reflection in its blind eyes.

For a while CoP stands looking at her bruises in the mirror, turning this way and that, giving me feedback. I'm making slow progress. We finish the moonshine. She dresses and leaves. She'll walk back home in the rain. She's unafraid of the streets. She's CoP, unafraid of everything. As she leaves I plant a kiss on her lips, and mine come away stained with lipstick. Her shit smell fills the air, soaks into my pores long after she's gone, incense burning at a roadside shrine.

ISSUE THREE:
JOY

poet's radio is excited tonight. Multiple voices babbling urgently, incomprehensible by the time they reach me. I lie on my mattress, the rain reduced to drips, my body buzzing, lazy and ready to sleep, and in this sleepstate listen to the radio static, parsing it. Meaning disengages from the noise. I pluck the Map that's floating in it. New coordinates.

White noise wakes me. A woman's screams. She's not so much screaming as saying the word "scream" over and over again with emotionless, flat intonation. Her baby emerged stillborn. I see the grave, pathetic and small. They exhume it the next day. The grave's empty.

Smoked and nutty, like something cooked in good butter. I lick my lips. Tasting it. Baby skewers.

Nothing to do in the afternoon, I go to the amusement park. The only one. *Joy*. I take three turns on the ferris wheel. One on the pirate ship. I ride a carousel horse. The park is free of its hectic night energy. Under the sun it's a sane place. Families stroll casually. I make friends with young girls and boys, buy them ice cream. We lick our cones in the food court, plastic chairs under faded umbrellas. We eat french fries wet with grease. A beggar asks me for a cigarette; I refuse.

The beggar stands behind me cursing, wishing me an ugly death, an emaciated child strapped across her chest. Her voice is hoarse like the voices of dead men. Every time she curses me, I smile a little more. Imagining in detail all the death she's wishing for me.

Death by drowning.

Death by fire.

Death by starvation.

Death by cancer.

Death by spirit possession (the spirits raping me from the *inside*).

Death by poison.

Death by head lice.

Here, I would die of a mechanical accident. A malfunctioning ride. The pirate ship careening off its tracks. It has happened before. Many times. FF and I were here, in line for a ride, when a baby fell flying off a ride. Someone caught it in the crowd. There were screams. I love this place.

Joy

The entrance fee is affordable, even cheap.

Next, I visit the woman, my neighbor to pay my respects. With a bouquet of white roses. She's veiled in black, half dead on her bed. I press the weeping husband to my chest, let him cry into my shirt. His dead child turned into protein.

It's happening everywhere. Dog, donkey, horse, chimp, all possible variety of human dead and dying. Placentas that had been buried in the ground.

Last night's transmission bore a new urgency. Those babbling mountain voices. Infectious. A new excitement rattles my veins, swells in my lymph. It's happening. Something, soon, will burst upon us like a storm cloud. Dissolve us as dust. I visit a shrine, chanting dark verses, swaying with the crowd.

Burning with the New Information, I spend the night in malevolent search. The Map covers my vision in a neon haze, my own secret smog. Everything I see I see through the smog. It's a select screening. Color coded. I follow the red blips, tracing a secret river. Here. Here. And here again, this street, that corner. They were here. Hordes of them. My breath catches at the image density. I was wrong in my previous calculations. Now I know what I'm looking at: a mass invasion, like leprosy or HIV.

I look at the food stall where I had ice cream and fries. I see the place where It stood, not two inches from the seat where I, that afternoon, had sat.

I look at the house of the mother whose baby was stillborn. It's red too. The Thing was here, right here, *in my neighborhood*, what was It doing here. My pulse quickens. My feet start tingling.

At dawn I stumble home. The city, at dawn, looks like some strange disease.

Q: her place; a movie. Q works at the history center, and when they throw out films she takes them home.

We're sitting on the sofa, there's popcorn and soda, talking about the film on screen and her work. Q likes her work. She likes, she says, to contribute to the preservation of *authenticity* and *truth*, and I remind her we're talking about reconstructions, copies. A cockroach in the corner of the room; Q won't let me kill it. She likes cockroaches. And she likes lizards. Theses are requirements that she fulfills. Q: I'm thinking again of telling her about the aliens, my aliens, the ones I hunt, but the primal secrecy stops me. Like her, I have orders. But my orders come from high up. Tense on the couch, I grind my knuckles into my knee. Look, Q takes my hand in hers, this scene. Then I'm looking at a sea monster rising up from the swelter of the sea, slimewaves rolling off its haunches, suction pods on the ends of its tentacles, the reverse of humanity's history. Q is telling me how old this film is. I am looking at the monster, picking its teeth with a skyscraper.

ISSUE FOUR:
THE SHADOW

The Shadow pulls away from a drainpipe, bandage ripping off a wound. Its robe and face and hands are black. Its eyes are glowing rubies. WE HAVE TO TALK, It transmits to me. Metal nails squeal down a chalkboard.

So talk, I transmit back, still walking. It drips after me. There's a wetness on the back of my neck, like there's a big dog breathing on me. The edges of my vision start to rip.

THERE ARE MORE OF THEM. YOU NEED TO INCREASE YOUR WORK HOURS. It sounds petulant. We're crossing the street in the middle of traffic. Car lights cut right through It. I'm doing my best, I reply. On the other side of the road, I pause to light a cigarette. Suddenly the air is cold and I don't know if it's me or the city.

I'm pinned to a tree by an invisible force. This close, The Shadow is Satan. Looking into Its eyes, I see a vision of Hell. It grips me with thin licks of flame. I faint and then recover, weakened but pleasurably, it feels nice like I've been in a sauna. The Shadow and I are seated under the tree.

The Shadow laughs: cars crash on the highway, trucks burst into flame. JUST A PRANK, It reassures me, pats my knee. I trust The Shadow. It is my Teacher, the first to have contacted me, my Initiator, Confidante.

WE ALL NEED HELP SOMETIMES, It offers a parting salvo. FIND THEM. DO AS I SAY.

Then It's gone. The ground where It sat is scorched lifeless. The air vibrates like a tuning fork.

The smog continues into the morning. From this greyness, the spires of the old city rise like soldiers or sentinels. Waiting. Waiting. I have a sudden intuition, but I switch it off. I'm not in the mood today.

DIRTIEST HOTEL IN THE WORLD

After The Shadow's visitation, very quiet on *poet's radio*. Murmurs and static kisses. I shack up in The Ice Hotel. It's the dirtiest hotel in the world.

A room on the 9th floor. It's large and has a double bed, two windows, a claw-foot bathtub in the attached bathroom. The carpet is puke. I touch the curtains and a shower of small cockroaches rains down on me. There are lizard eggs on the bookshelf. I look at the mattress and see its infestation. I pick up the phone, order room service. *001*, I tell them. A bottle of gin, and a bottle of tonic. I put the drinks in the minifridge, lie down to sleep.

The bedbugs feast on me, but I don't care. My skin is a hardened tool. I wake up buzzing, refreshed. In bed, I drink a cool gin and tonic. The rim of the glass is smudged red with a woman's lipstick. I place my lips neatly over the stain.

The view from my window is majestic, sweeping, sublime. The city is a pattern of impotent lights, suffocating under smog. I stare at it. It stares back at me with blind, occluded eyes.

On TV, a singer singing the cursed song. I'm amazed: he has nerves, guts, incredible daring. Everyone who sings this song dies the next day. It's a love song. Tortured love. Like all love, tainted. He's singing the song for a live audience. There's total silence, complete absorption. This man committing suicide. I mute the show. I came here to work. I make myself another drink.

I spread out my things on the desk. My news clippings. My printouts. My photographs. *My dossier.* I review my journal, resolving its code—my code, in my hand and of my invention—into meaning again. My log of everything *poet's radio* said. The past is a swamp that lathers my organs. I feel delirious and at ease. Unthreatened. And unafraid.

The original message falls open in front of me.

It's a polaroid. 9cm x 9cm. Black and white. A series of telescoping polygons. Rectangles and squares. Black at the edges, ceding to grey and then white by the center— the middle is a single square, just a pixel, absolutely white. The Mothership. She. The geometric center. The Absolute. The rest is radiation, her transmissions.

Beneath it, someone's scrawled in red pen—

West of the old city. East of the sun.

Then, as now, I fall into it. Its creamy greys. Its whites like the whites of eyes. Its warm, inviting black. Sometimes I think this is it, the reality of Them, a palette of feelings and experience given tactile form. My liver is happy with this idea. My kidney. And my spleen.

The approach of the sightlines. The almost-perfect overlap. We are waiting for this. We are trying. To recover that moment when things almost aligned—and when they align, when every event is perfect in its coordinate, preordained, precise, when I and the aliens encounter each other in such a way, such a state, the mystery of this will, like mist, be lifted. I have been promised this. It has been promised to me.

I am a coordinate, I know. I'm hunting aliens, but I'm not hunting them for me.

Thrum of bass, I follow a scent to the dancefloor. There's a limp crowd, noodles. Something malevolent flickers in me. I'm dancing with a woman. A woman is dancing with me. I bite into her neck, softly, firmly, bite like an insect, pincers sinking in, blood on my lips—

– someone taps me on the shoulder, and it's CoP! She! She's with someone—a man in a black suit—but it's me she's looking at. I take her hand. She rescues me.

We sit in a booth in the back of the dancefloor. Shrimp on ice. Me, CoP, and her men in black suits. 3 of them, sunglasses although it's dark inside. She preempts a kiss by eating a shrimp.

CoP has a scar in her left eyebrow and her face, botched surgery, melts often, like now, the flesh of her chin and cheeks sagging in clumps. She pats them back into shape. They fall down again. She pats them back. They droop. When her face droops, CoP looks like an imposter in a mask, except behind the mask there's nothing, not even nothing, viscera and blood and bone.

Later, her clients gone, CoP and I go back to my room. It's past midnight, a weeknight. CoP sits on a chair and takes off her shoes. It's been a long day, she says. Under pressure of speech, her lower lip dips a few inches to the left.

CoP I met in the old city, in Meat Market. Everybody loves Meat Market. Simply everyone. I was there on a tip, looking for an alien. It had been sighted in a gutter outside a butcher's house, injured, some kids had been throwing rocks at it. When I got there, it was gone. Just a faint green slime where it must have been. While I was examining the site—taking photos and samples of the slime—a woman came running out of the house. Her face was on fire.

CoP and I are twinsouls.

ISSUE SIX:
MEN IN RED

The walk back to my house is dreary, chalky. Nightbirds, big racket. As I turn into my neighborhood, the whistle of a train cuts the air. It's the new train. The one they built through the center of the city. I imagine a figure framed in the doorway, outlined in yellow light. He's pushed from behind.

It's in a dumpster. I feel it before I see It. The blue body; the oval eyes. Its skin emits a hot glow.

We are face to face now. We make eye contact—I am looking into its eyes, and something passes from it to me. I swallow something tactile in my throat, prickly like thorns on a rose. The air is buzzing, filled with bees. I block it out. I screen all sound. My world contracts to the alien immediately before me.

I snap on the black gloves and stretch out my hands. The space between us turns hard. I've hit an invisible barrier, then I've passed through. Along my wrists, a line of blue heat.

There's a blast and I'm knocked backwards. Fly several feet through the air before landing on my back, snapping muscles and minor bones. Everything is bright light and noise.

Thump of helicopters. Men's voices shouting. Radio static.

The light resolves into a pair of floodlights, trained from the bottom of the choppers. The choppers hover above the dumpster, let down lines of rope. Men in red suits slink down the ropes. They look like carpenter ants.

The men in red surround the dumpster in an oval, two AK-47s per man, their suits are sleek and well-fitting, tailor-made for sure. Tie pin on every tie. Red brogues. A gas mask over every face. The choppers continue to hover overhead, floodlights trained on the dumpster, on the alien cowering in the trash.

One of the men steps forward, breaking formation. A floodlight scooches onto him. He flicks his wrist in the air and a ziploc bag appears in it. With a pair of tongs, he grabs the alien by the waist and drops it into the ziploc, which he ziplocs. The alien's upside down in the bag, large eyes at the bottom, hooved feet by the zip.

The men in red lean their guns against their legs and applaud primly. Then they're gone in 3 seconds, back up the ropes and into the helicopters, the floodlights flicking off, the helicopters stealth now, soundless now. There's a final hissing sound.

Plumes of white phosphor uncoil in the air.

I climb out of the gutter where I fell, run away.

So I'm not alone! *I'M NOT ALONE*. In my bedroom, broken back, I yell into **poet's radio**, defying physics, defying everything, I'm bleeding from my nose. It's silent on **poet's radio**. It's dawn when I fall asleep.

Pain wakes me and I go to the hospital.

Across the uncharted wastes of space, M Hospital. Three people to every bed. Flies in the operating room, piss on the floor. The doctor who sees me spanks my ass.

I take a taxi back home. The cabbie shares his opium with me, which I use medicinally.

I paint a red *M* on my forehead. My defiant gesture, my gesture of rebellion.

ISSUE SEVEN:
THE CLOWN

So, have you seen her lately? Hanging from the ceiling fan, he's in my house before me.

The Clown.

I shut the door again and leave. A squeak and he's right there next to me, turning cartwheels and following me. We go to a café. I order coffee, he orders juice.

So, how's she doing? Have you seen her lately? He scratches the paint on his cheek and repeats himself. A fly slips into his mouth.

No, you idiot, she's dead. I answer him. The walls throw the words back at me. Dead dead dead, they echo. Gleefully, d e a d, d e a d, deadddddddddd.

Oh.

What's that thing on your back?

Our drinks arrive. I tell The Clown I broke my back. He tsks and orange juice dribbles down his lip.

How did she die did you kill her.

I throw my plate at him. It shatters a few inches before it reaches him. Plucking shards off his shirt, he says,

She was my sister you know. That counts for something. Blood counts for something. His eyes turn into hallucinations. Hypnotize me. She was my sister and she counted for something. It's too bad she loved you. It's too bad I love you too.

I snap out of my hypnosis. What, I ask him. What did you say? But he's giggling now, and wiggling his bright yellow tongue at me, Show tonight come see me. He puts a ticket on the table then cartwheels out the door, leaving me to pick up the tab.

Walk through the smog to the circus, follow the spire of the tent. The circus tent is visible for miles, strung with red lights. It's pitched in an empty lot, the ground they use for fairs and carnivals and shows. There's a crowd. Lightness, laughter. I buy a stick of cotton candy. It's fluffy and blue.

Someone takes the ticket and candy from my hand, and I enter the tent.

The Unlucky Circus!

Curly font on a bright blue banner, strung across the center of the tent. Tiered seating along the walls of the tent. It's a full house. I squeeze in between strangers, bucket of popcorn on their knees. The butter makes my fingers wet.

Ringmaster's a man with an egg-shaped face, shiny bald pate, lips razorthin, red and smiling. He's wearing a sleek black suit, looking dapper, looking smart. A whip in his hand and a loudspeaker, with which he bellows at the crowd. Announces the show. First there is the national anthem that the band belts out. The band: fat men just behind the ring.

The first act is the acrobats, women swinging through the air, holding hands, switching places on trapezes. Parallelograms in the air. No safety nets. It's amazing, watching their graceful deaths. The circus is a family business; acrobatic through the bloodline. This new girl, for instance, the one *turning cartwheels* in the air. She is the daughter of the acrobat who died last year. The couple next to me point, whisper. There's an aura to her. Aura of death, which is of course a stench. Her breasts are petite, wisps barely there, wrapped in gauze beneath her shirt. She doesn't die today.

The pinheads look like rats so their act is called The Rats. Do rat stuff on stage. Scurry about on all fours. Rats don't have an incest taboo. Put some rats in a cage without food and they'll practice cannibalism. Every microencephalopath in the city is donated here, the Circus takes them, here they have family, familiars, metal caps forced on the head to accentuate the rat skull shape.

There are children, painted blue, cannon balls for the human cannon. A blue child pops across the stage, high in the sky, streak of blue against the tent top. Nervous laughter. Jeers of glee. I'm amazed at this *temerity*.

But one wouldn't expect any less from *The Unlucky Circus*.

Snake eater with a snake in his right hand, coke in his left. He pulls the snake through his teeth, rips out the meat, waves the empty snake skin in the air. I've talked to him. He says it tastes like chicken, goes down very nicely with coke. Never Pepsi, only coke; coke really makes a snake pop. Smear of blood on his hands and mouth. I love this man! I stand up on my seat and cheer.

The circus is in town three times a year. After the show I walk among the tents sampling food, trying snacks. The circus has its own generator, booming in the distance. This way they never have a blackout and the show, which must go on, does go on. Look at this crowd; various; old; young; confused and with lights in their eyes, there are rides in the grounds behind the tents. Rusted metal frames a man moves with his shoulders, his shoulders give out every year. He replaces them with metal caps, a new pair of caps each year.

Great show! I find The Clown in his tent, hug him. His face is wet with sweat. **Thank you for coming,** The Clown whispers, a scratching in his throat like a taloned thing stuck in there, sharpening its nails against his cilia. He's emotional from another successful show. I want to linger but the manager is here, man I've never seen, he has needle eyes, I say hello and leave. Outside again, fumes of the generator.

FF and I used to come here. She used to bring me to these circus shows. Now, alone, I feel her presence like a bloody mist. Her brother The Clown is here; I know he feels it too. I float around the grounds, lonely in a crowd, feeling levity, feeling free. There's a freak show behind me, but I don't go inside. I feel enraged, totally satisfied and well pleased.

ISSUE EIGHT:
NEW BEGINNINGS

I'm the last person to leave the circus for the night, straggling around the empty ground. I follow the stars home. It's a grand map. Even clearer than my veins, more articulate. A star blinks overhead, vanishes: heat death of the universe.

I want to sleep the sleep of a thousand years.

The message is waiting for me when I go looking for it. On cigarette paper, stuffed in a drainpipe. In the public restrooms. In the same handwriting. Smelling, as always, of piss.

Unexpected Interference. Interference Unexpected. Unexpected Interference.

It continues in an infinite loop. It's a broken satellite. I turn the paper over, write my reply.

I deposit my message back in its place. Replacing the one I picked up.

My secret network, my network of friends.

Invisible, geometric sequence. We resolve into a telescoping series. I'm sure of it. We articulate something beautiful and sublime, we become

The Thing that is beautiful

The Thing that is never diseased

Meanwhile, **poet's radio**. It chastises me. When it finally speaks. There was *an interruption in the flow.* And you were *unequal* to it. I stare at these lines. I write them on my bedroom wall. They write themselves on my intestines.

Staring at it, I feel murderous. Abused. Explosive like an immanent device.

I pick up a tire iron. I visit The Tailor.

I remember the men in red. I remember their handsome tailoring.

He's the best of the best, our finest tailor. His shop's near the old city. Adjacent. Amber glow of prestige. I stand in his doorway, slap the tire iron in my left hand. His customers see me and leave. The Tailor rises slowly from his seat, old, arthritic, lifts his hands above his head, starts to speak.

I clock him above the right temple. A soft knock. He falls against the wall, splattering blood.

Red suits, I say. Terror spreads across his face.

He won't speak.

You're scared of them, I tell him, but you should be scared of me.

I rip his tongue out with my hand. I pin the tongue to the door of his shop, a red and slimy thing. An evident symbol. Signal for the times.

Blackout. Middle of the afternoon.

I lie under an unmoving fan. Supine. Lizards crawl over my stomach and chest.

Failure. Its bitter taste.

I begin my studies anew. Scrap the falsehoods of the past. Burn my notebooks.

This will be a New Era.
I will make it so.

I drink bitter drinks.

I laugh into the queer night.

ISSUE NINE:
B, THE DETECTIVE

My first new move: I enlist the support of B, The Famous Detective.

She's wearing tall leather boots, black jacket, white wifebeater. She's smoking a cigarette. We meet at a tea stall. She doesn't offer me a cigarette.

I want you to find and follow a series of men in red, I tell her, leaning in close though no one's listening, They're a group or a coterie. A cadre. A secret body. I want you to find them and report to me. Their actions. Their activities. Names, photos, and addresses.

B rubs her thumb and index finger.
I hand her a wad of cash.

The tea boy fills our cups with more tea. He's wearing just a tattered grey vest. It's hot in the sun. I realize I've sweated through my collared shirt; it's turning translucent, see-through like vapor.

B's the best in the business. Everyone knows this. Her eyes are shot with liquor though it's noon. Fingernails red like rust, long. B's a bus crawler, day stalker. She rides the school buses, picking up schoolgirls. Her house is a mansion. Guarded by pit bulls. The girls never want to go and never want to leave. B hacks out a gob of spit. It lands on my bright new shoes.

See you when I see you. B's voice is nails. Gotta go, her eyes follow a girl as she speaks. The girl's getting off a bus. She's walking home from school. White uniform. The back of her shirt is wet and smudged pink, her period's bleeding through her underwear. B throws down pennies for her tea, disappears.

I have never needed to contract B before. These are new times. In this altered time, I am extending my network of friends. It's a risky, frisky business. My kidney tells me I can trust B.

Where is The Shadow when I want him? I could use some help right now. I scream at the night. But there is no reaching The Shadow, no means of finding him, we're not connected, I know this, I've always known this. But still.

It flickers on and off in front of me, the eyes of this city, its light.

The Tailor is back in business already. I passed his shop this morning, on my way to B. I'm very unhappy with myself, skills I never learnt. How to torture. I note this in the notebook of my deficiencies.

As I walked by his shop, the Tailor turned to look at me. No bandages, no sign of damage. He gleamed malevolently, rubbing in his victory, *sticking out the new tongue between his teeth.*

My skin, at this new insult, erupts in a rash.

The woman whose child was stillborn. She wakes me in the night, her screams. She tried to kill herself. Commotion in the street. I go out, I'm told she locked herself in her bathroom, drank toilet cleaner. Detergent. And other stuff.

Someone rescues her. There's an ambulance.

Bored, I go to the movie store. It's open all night. College kid behind the counter, pimply and thin. The sign outside is neon, flickering, shooting sparks sometimes.

I pick up some unmarked tapes. They're snuff tapes. I watch them alone in my living room, take notes, multifarious forms of torture, electrode to the nipple, recorded screams playing over me.

FF and I had a habit. Movies from the movie store, then burgers, fries and coke. My place or hers. Throughout the night all over us, wash of technicolor, recorded sound. We watched slasher flicks and B movies. Horror films direct to DVD.

We were techno lovers. I still see her sometimes.

Those are my best nights. Sometimes I'm almost whole.

Strange blue bodies in the news. It's in the back pages. I clip these items out neatly, very neatly. Deposit in my dossier.

The headlines are crowded; a new epidemic. Sneaky like the flu.

City on lockdown. In theory.

I imagine myself as a virus, a prion.

I could burrow right into the *genes*. I would *be* these genes. All secrets would be open to me.

Electric, I remember certain feelings. The feeling of whooshing through air, lightweight, mobile, and free.

ISSUE TEN:
MOON MARKET

My sessions are more violent now. More focused. I'm all the time concentrating. Walking the streets with my eyes to the ground. Nerves firing. Skin alive. Hair prickling.

I study each electron, gather samples of air. I shut my eyes at random spots. Send out heat flares.

Listen to the thrum, beat of blood, all the sounds trapped in things. I'm good at this. Coaxing voices out of wood, releasing the past. The trees like talking to me. We have long, extended chats.

I was in Moon Market when it blew up. I wasn't the one who bombed it. But I knew it was coming.

The ground started to shiver. That was how I knew. And the sky, the birds. They could have seen it in the birds. *Always look at the birds,* doesn't everyone know this? For a moment I stood still, in the center of the market, looking upwards at the birds. Their cries drowned by the market, its noise. Then I flew on.

Blood in the drains. Blood in the taps. I run myself a shower, and the water came out red.

In the morning I clip the report of the bombing from the newspaper. Add it to my incidental file. It's slim. I'm severe about my clippings. Every morning I sit on the verandah in my slippers, and review my incidental dossier.

A kite falls by my feet, carried by the wind. I pick it up. The string is hard with powdered glass. It cuts me and I bleed.

Something melancholy in me. I'm mourning something, mourning her, mourning a thing I'm not aware of. I go for a walk. My cut finger stings.

A donkey dying in the street.

I go to the remains of Moon Market, shards on the street, everything starting back up again. FF and I used to come here. I go to the corner with the ice cream stand.

I eat a vanilla cone.

Other flavors: vanilla-chocolate, chocolate, cherry, vanilla-chocolate-cherry swirl.

The ice cream man chats with me. He asks me about my friend, he means FF. We talk about things. What happened in Moon Market. The weather, the constant smog.

He tells me about the thing he saw yesterday. Right here, he says, pointing at my feet, right here where you're standing now. I saw a strange thing. A child, but it was blue. The child's body was totally blue. The man said he'd fled. He hadn't stopped for a good look. But I knew better. As he talks his eyes shimmer. The glitch is dancing in his eyes.

I drop my ice cream in the trash. The Shadow is gliding next to me. It's in a coat that flaps as It moves, red on the inside, black on the out. Top hat. Gloves. With one hand It scatters cards on the street. An ace. Diamond. Kings and Queens. YOU'RE A FOOL.

INCREASE YOUR WORK HOURS. FIND THEM. DO AS I SAY. The words unfurl in front of me in cursive. There's nervousness inside me. Look, I stutter, Why didn't you tell me there were others?

The Shadow pauses. Everything freezes. I feel ice form along my surface. The Shadow is all I can see. Its faceless face. Coming closer.

THERE AREN'T. These words get trapped in my skin.

Q asks me why I'm holding a joker. I offer it to her: a gift.

Q and I at a restaurant. It's in the new District, the one they built the train for. It zips residents from the District into the city and out again; near and far, far and near at the same time. Safe distances. The joker I've given Q is hanging from her pocket, sticking its tongue out at me. And juggling pink juggling balls.

The railway system is collapsing, I know. I know. I don't recognize the names on the menu. I order what Q orders. Each minute I spend in this airconditioned room, I fall a little more out of my skin.

We found a secret room in the Fort, Q tells me. The Fort is in the old city, monument, tourist trap. I have been there on a million dates. Our food arrives: charred vegetables, something clotted to drink. A secret room? I ask. Q tells me: A team of archaeologists discovered it. It is *fascinating* and *alarming*, but she won't tell me why. You have to see it to believe it—so it's settled. We pick a date. I pop a piece of zucchini in my mouth.

Q asks me what I've been doing, if I've found a job yet. The question makes me pause; I don't like it. I don't like to lie to my friends. Q. Q's frank eyes. I look at the table. At the grain of its wood. The evening air is cool, sweet. Someone enters and then exits the cafe.

I tell Q I haven't found a job yet.

A black crow perches on the back of a chair. I look at it. It looks at me. It's an ordinary crow. I think of my friends: Q, B, CoP. I even consider The Shadow my friend, though we're separated by entire planes of reality. Q pays the bill though I don't want her to. Dear Q. We take separate trains home. The floor of the train unsteady beneath my feet...I have heard horror stories, of the floor of the train falling clean away, death on the express.

Blackout. On the verandah, putrid heat. Smell of imminent rain. The sky descending.

A crow caws and I remember FF.

FF. My Femme Fatale. They killer her. Who killed her? They did it because they could. And because concepts, when they are before their time, *must* suffocate, *must* die. They're sacrificed. Like she. Within conditions of impossibility   which conditions   these conditions

Exhausted from a long day, I curl up on the ground, fall asleep.

I'm enveloped by queasy dreams. In one of them, a crow lands on my chest and begins feasting on me. It dips its beak into my sockets like into an ink well, eating my eyes.

ISSUE ELEVEN:
ANOTHER ALIEN

I wake to a beeping alarm. Neither low nor high. An even pitch, one single frequency. I ooze into the red hole of *poet's radio*.

These are urgent, excited messages. I scrawl at a furious rate. The garbled distorted voices, overlapping, canceling and amplifying, layered with the sound of the hills. It unfurls a lengthy exposition, which I collect on the plane of the page.

The hunt is afoot. I race through the night. Wrapped in the smog I am the smog.

Seeping through the night. Dispossessed. My antennae poised and quivering. Picking up signals. Reading the signs. A dead man hunting for signs of life.

poet's radio was right. Things are lively tonight.

Concepts are organic matter, like cells. Pausing in a gutter to examine a body, I dwell on this. My thoughts, her thoughts. It's just a child. I turn her over with my shoe. There is drool bubbling on the corner of her lips. I smell it. It smells rancid.

A bullet clips my ear.

The car overturns, wheels spinning in the air like cockroach legs. Burning rubber. Petrol smell. Sound of a machete dragging across concrete.

I observe the carnage from a rooftop, lying flat on my belly. My vision is distorted. Things are red. I'm looking through a heat maze. These bodies are magnesium flares. I squint through it. White fog. Then. That. In the distance. A rupture in the air.

I'm there, sucked through a vacuum tube that shoots me to the other side of the signal. The street is quiet, sleeping. She's beneath a banyan tree. It's been injured. I crouch down near his alien frame. Forgetting my caution. It's a small blue body, exactly like the others.

With my index finger, I touch its protruding belly. It's hot. My finger comes back scorched; burning with light. The thing is looking at me with its large, oval eyes. Calm. Curious. I sense a humming, like bees. It wriggles its fingers and toes. The alien's mouth spreads in a smile. Something begins to come out of it, a bug, fat and disgorged, like a cockroach, or even a lizard, blackish and, also, smiling.

The moment pauses, and distends.

The following has been schooled in me. Implanted in me. I tap the air and a panel appears. Key the code onto its fat red buttons, the switchboard of the cosmos. A cone of cloudy white light pops over the alien, encapsulating it, then they both disappear. It's a slow fade. The blue alien lightens, loses color, becomes translucent, then finally disappears, shucked up by the cone of light. It's gone into the Portal. I know of The Portal.

It transports through disintegration. That is what happened to me: my cells were uncombined, then recombined. I was on the other side. In the presence of The Syndicate. I experienced The Syndicate as a black field—a plane of darkness over an otherwise even bright—the darkness deep like velvet, and undulant.

Then when I returned, I could hear **poet's radio.** And the interim is a false memory.

I wake up on my back, in my bed. Pigeons burring outside my window. I lie in the damp heat, completely still. Tasting my sweat.

I log my alien in my notebook. I give it a
serial number and unique ID.

I think of the thing that was coming out of
it. A lizard. Or a cockroach. Dark in a blue
body. Fat and slimy. I wish I had touched
it. I think of The Syndicate. The Syndicate
is an affect in me. Like a force field.

I think of The Syndicate often, but these thoughts are never good for me.

ISSUE TWELVE:
B'S PLEASURE PALACE

Come on, CoP says, takes my hand, takes me walking down the street. It's the middle of the afternoon; the air smells like petrol. Like an imminent explosion.

The sky's thick with birds. This has been happening for a while. A long time now. There have been birds in the sky, all species, odd hours. It's a mass exodus. I watch them carefully. I want to read their pattern. There is a pattern. Yesterday, I saw a starling murmuration. This was right before the murder, when the lady whose child was stillborn was found dead, at dawn, she had been hacked with an axe. I could smell the blood in my bed. It filtered through my dreams.

Then I saw the husband at the tea stall, having tea. Teacup smudged with the blood on his hands.

CoP won't let me stop, she's impatient, imperious. Ever since she lost her face, she's been an expert of the streets. Fearless. Completely unafraid. This is a dangerous way to be.

A crow shits near me. The stream of shit misses me by an inch, CoP laughs. Her laugh is parched like her. She's taking me to see B, though I don't tell her why. I should trust B and I do, but still. I remember ten fingers poking from a drain. It was raining. The fingers looked like fat worms in the haze.

We walk through the maze of the city. CoP guides me. We pass the street where I caught the alien. It's been razed. Dust and rubble. The skin behind my knees erupts in a rash. Come on, CoP says, seeing me flag. She buys me a bag of nuts. I eat these. She takes me to where B lives. I have only ever heard of it.

B lives in a mansion. Guarded by pit bulls, they yelp as we approach. A manservant runs out, subdues them, walks us in. So: our approach was anticipated. This makes me smile. B: she knows everything.

We sit in her living room. Chandelier, bookcases, black leather sofa. Manservant brings biscuits and tea. The lady, he says with his eyes on the floor, will be with you shortly.

I tune in. Moans and whimpers, so much pleasure it makes the walls vibrate. This is B's Pleasure Palace. It's infamous. They want it gone, but no one messes with B. She's an infinite lifeform

A cuckoo clock cuckoos on the wall.

B's in a silk nightgown, hair tousled, skin sweaty. Smudge of pink across her lips. Welcome, welcome, B says, lazy, slinking onto the sofa across from us, waving away manservant who has discreetly appeared, Welcome to my home! She spreads her hands in a generous gesture. CoP and I say thanks. Their eyes meet, B and CoP. Something flickers between them. Suddenly I'm aware of past histories, preparing to flare.

Any news?, I ask B. No, she says tonelessly, and I know it's a lie. The thing in my head begins to buzz.

The men in red, I begin to say, my antagonists, but I'm interrupted by—

— a naked girl running down the steps. She jumps in B's lap. She's maybe 16. Her pubic hair is delicate and fine.

B curls a hand in it. The girl purrs like a cat, nibbles B's fingers. B whistles. Manservant appears with tumblers, ice and whiskey. I take mine straight. The girl; she's told her parents she's in school. It's a lovely lie. Meanwhile she's here. The whole city knows it. Everyone resents B her raucous pleasure. I remember the pit bulls. And the snipers, hiding out of sight.

Make yourself comfortable, B says, offers me a cigarette. It's a banned brand. The smoke filters through my lungs and poisons them. I feel decadent. Another girl joins the first. They want to drink with B. They're sitting on both sides of her like baby snakes, drugged with sex. B licks each pair of lips. Then she snaps her fingers and the girls are gone like wisps of smoke.

Don't come here again, B says to me, quiet now, all business now, Don't come here asking about the men in red.

B looks at CoP and the thing flickers between them again. Shoots out sparks. Glows redhot. B's frowning. I've seen you somewhere, she says, haven't I seen you somewhere before? Maybe, replies CoP, voice all drugged and sleepy, everyone's seen me somewhere before.

The men in red, I interrupt, pour more whiskey, are my enemies. I need to know. I need to know everything about them, *everything*, please B. Please!

The men in red know everything, B and CoP intone together, and no one knows anything about the men in red. Their lapped voices reverberate. I'm struck speechless. Feeling like a fool.

Then B's taken my hand, and CoP's too. She takes us to her underground lair. Sex Dungeon. So the rumors were true. It's layers and layers. Tunneled by groundhogs. Endlessly circuitous, iterations of itself, dead ends, repeats. It's designed to be unnavigable. The ground is soft and shifts beneath our feet. We wear gas masks on our faces. In a second I'm flooded with ghosts. The ghosts are strips of ultraviolet blue. Like light over jaundiced babies.

This here, B is pointing to a cul-de-sac, is a special room. I discern it: it's like a cave, dark and deceptive, and inside it there are living bodies, still alive, chained to the walls, moans and whimpers. I look at the bodies in awe. The price of pleasure, I know, I know. I feel a sense of warm kinship for B. We exit the cul-de-sac, go back to her living room.

In her living room again, I tell B she's off the hook. She is the best detective, but she's not employed anymore. B looks at me; her lips curl into a smile. I know that smile. It makes me shy.

CoP stays behind. I leave her sitting next to B, the air between them fulgurating with something hidden, obscene, and malign. It makes me nervous. I walk home alone, comforted by the dark night.

In my room, I pace and take stock. Time has been on my side so far, but now we're on the other side. I sense it. It's a feeling.

I have been slow in several respects. Hesitating. Now all my pauses are catching up to me. I step into the shower and think of this. My weaknesses. My many failings.

The alien had been sitting there, bleeding, for maybe hours before I got to it. What if I *had not* got to it? What would happen next? The razor falls from my fingers. I am shivering and weak.

Where is it now, the alien? With The Syndicate. At the thought of The Syndicate, a synapse fires in my brain. I lose a reflex. And gain a new one in return.

Sometimes in the shower, I watch my body turn on me. Shampoo swirling between my toes. It looks like webbing. My belly button protrudes. I was a sickly child, often ill.

A lizard slinks along the edge of the wet tile floor, disappears into the drain.

FF and I were made to be. This is why we could not be. *Some things are meant to happen*, this is a temptation. I think of synchronicity sometimes, strangeness in time. Supernatural seconds. Eternities that transpire in seconds. Kinks in fabrics, blackhole time.

FF was a concept ahead of her time. The two of us. FF and me. We used to spend white nights together. And then a pillar of salt. In the pouring rain.

I remember how I found her. Dead on my bed. Humiliated. A lizard on her butt. On her face a glasglow smile.

Someone wanting to *communicate* with me. I tear a hole in the wall with my nails. Feeling feverish. Feeling despair.

My task sometimes feels too vast for me, after all it is of cosmic proportions. Mere me.

I go to the shrine of the saint. The one who watches over this city. No one sleeps hungry here and it's all because of him. He has been dead a thousand years. I sway with the rest of them. Drunk in various ways. Chanting strange verses. Words I don't understand. Thick lines of incense.

I rip my shirt, tear through the streets. I'm craving a hit again. Banging on locked doors. Stumbling through streets dissolving in the rain. Then I'm a line of red, staining the sidewalk cracks.

ISSUE THIRTEEN: PREMONITIONS

Q and I go to the Fort. It's crowded as always, plus we picked a weekend, Q off from her job. It's evening and the heat's slid a little. There is a records room in this Fort, an archive, built into what used to be a tomb. A woman was interred in its walls; they've hollowed all the walls but not found her. Then it was a stable for imperial horses. Now it's this, an official record room.

We walk through the Fort, casual, its crumbling walls, Q telling me about the secret room, the progress they've made with it. We buy cigarettes and cotton candy from a wooden stall. The man has no teeth, only gums. Corroded with sugar, tobacco.

Children run around us, screaming. In the sky, several kites. I point upwards: look, kites. These are banned. As soon I've pointed they're gone.

Q follows the arc of my finger. She lands on a star, still faint in the evening sky.

The carcass of the royal Fort. It's pitted with significant holes. Tap a brick here, touch this crack, and a panel of the wall turns elegantly, the angle still precise through the centuries, we're in the secret room. Q guides my hand along fake surfaces. Then we descend there. We reach it through the wall.

There are skeletons chained to the wall. Peeking from an open jaw, a rat's ass. Things stiffen in me, and burr. Mixing signals. Something happened here.

Q tells me it's a Torture Room, she says "espionage," I hear her and don't hear. **poet's radio**, buzzing business. My ankles click against each other. I'm listening; I'm listening.

To the breathing of the walls.

There were aliens here. Many aliens. A multitude such as I've never encountered. **poet's radio** bursts into frenzy. There are alarms, burning through me. What happened here? Something important. Something I don't understand. Straw crunches beneath our feet as we walk through its damp depths, Q and I, inhaling mold and spores and other, strange viruses. She pauses in the center of the room. Special Torture Room. There's a breaking wheel, stake, stretching racks, compression tools, implements I've seen before in dreams.

I was here. I've walked these floors. I was here, in this room. I lie down on the curve of the wheel, the horrible circumference, my spine aligning as it aligned once before.

The ceiling above me. That stain. My eyelids start to twitch, my pupils assuming the shape of the stain.

FF is next to me, lying on the breaking wheel, her jaw broken by a thousand slashes. I rise screaming. I'm still standing there, next to Q, arms folded, listening attentively. Q; she turns to me, and her head revolves. She is looking at me upside down, lips still moving, chin pointed upwards at the ceiling, forehead pressed against her neck, torn edges from which drip a foaming black ooze.

In the sunlight, on the stairs. Listening to a wooden flute. Drinking moonshine. Q's arm in mine.

When we make love it's night, on her rooftop, bricks rubbing against my skin, sloughing it.

ISSUE FOURTEEN:
THE MASSACRE

The massacre begins in the old city. The air buzzes with low-flying planes, dropping lines of white phosphor. It's a white wall descending from the sky, killing everything. People stream out of their houses, trying to escape through the old city's nine gates. The snipers shoot them. The snipers rise out of the ground, instantaneous blood ballet. Precision shots, one for each moving body. When no one comes out any more, the army moves in, poring through the narrow streets like a line of red ants. The massacre progresses via right angles and straight lines. It spreads through the city like an itch. The circus tent collapses in flames. Its fumes mix with the smog, which is covering everything. The freaks are trampled by the trapeze artists who are fed to the lion. The snake eater is eaten by the snakes. The pirate ship in the amusement park snaps off its railings. Hurtles into the crowd, a missile. Systematic breakdown; sabotage. Blackout everywhere. Every light bulb blows out. Tinkle of the glass falling from street lamps. People fall in clumps like flies. The army marches through streets thick with bodies, heavy boots, gas masks on faces. They fire up the brick kilns, bundle bodies into it. From the smokestacks, human smoke. Catching in the machinery, bits of human bone. The rattle of machine guns shreds the night. Bulleting smiles across dead faces. It ends at dawn.

ISSUE FIFTEEN: SILENCE

Then there's perfect silence. Just the hiss of white phosphor continuous from the sky, whispering flame, murmur of night insects.

It's a grey dawn. The city is a landfill, crushed and smoldering.

I wake to the scene. The smell of blood presses like a vice, thick, inescapable, rotting. I see the men in red outside my window, hosing down a street. Washing organs and blood into the drains. Erasing evidence.

It's a slow cleanup. There are dead bodies on every street.

Cargo for the sea.

Looking for CoP, I find her on a streetlamp. Tied to the pole. Body burned with a thousand cigarette burns. Mouth open. Tongue missing. Eyes gone. Flies feasting on her empty eye holes.

B as well. Her mansion is rubble. Pit bulls dead. Manservant missing. She's somewhere buried in the rubble. An arm, poking through the bricks; hers. I dig her out with my hands. She's mutilated too. Bald. Cheeks open. Legs terminating at the knees. Mouth contorted in a horrible scream.

I bury my friends in my backyard. I put flowers on their fresh graves, water them with my tears. A chemical ache is spreading through me. I shiver uncontrollably.

The massacre is missing from the news. Like every massacre, this massacre never happened at all.

I remember the men in red. They with the fire truck, washing away evidence. I remember their motions in the dawnlight, confident, silent and profound.

I know everything now.

Two things happen simultaneously. The knowledge of the men in red comes to me, and **poet's radio** shuts off.

Radio silence. Zero transmission. No more messages. Nothing. My cells stop buzzing. Antennae collapse. The world is surfaces, again, just surface, and nothing behind. I rest my palm against the bathroom wall and it's held there, solid, static, by a world that is closing its doors to me.

Futile. Despair. I claw at the air as if to snatch the messages out of it but nothing happens, I'm unhurt, my nails find no traction in the air.

They've shunted me off the Frequency.

The Shadow said goodbye in a dream. In this dream, The Shadow was looking at me with disappointed, bleeding eyes. Its eyes, which are red holes, were dripping blood onto my hands and feet. A sadness passed from it to me. I digested it. It settled in me. The Shadow's mouth was moving, it was saying something—important—a thing of final significance, but all I could hear was myself, waking up. I woke with blood on my hands as if I had *killed* The Shadow, or as if The Syndicate had hurt it.

Then I never saw The Shadow again. This was our final goodbye, and it happened in a dream.

I walk the streets and the streets are silent. High noon, asleep in the afternoon. Unresonant. I glide along surfaces; surfaces are all that remain to me.

The city is a chilling queen. Back from the dead and back to life again. Today the markets and cinemas opened. Death in every face.

At night I burn my fingertips with matches. Reproducing something that won't be reproduced. The effects of the contact. What it felt like. When I touched alien skin.

Light a fire in the verandah. Pages from my dossier. Page by page. Slowly. Itemized. Dossier and incidental file. One thing at a time. I feed it all to the flame.

On the bathroom floor I break down and cry.

ISSUE SIXTEEN:
DOUBLE CROSS

Something flutters down from the roof, gently falls on me. It's a playing card. A joker. Juggling pink juggling balls. It's the card The Shadow gave me.

She was my sister and that counts for something. The Clown is peeling from the corner, turning into cards, there are playing cards flying all over the bathroom, hitting the walls, hitting the commode and sink, hitting me on the nose and chin. His voice issues from all the cards at once, tinny, high-pitched, **She was my sister but that doesn't mean everything.**

I look in the mirror and The Clown is in the mirror, grinning at me. **It means I loved her but it doesn't mean I liked her.**

Now he's in the bathtub. Running himself a bath. Lifting one leg out of the bubbles, then the other, singing and soaping himself. **We were in cahoots. Right from the beginning! What's happened to you, friend? What's happened to your friends!** He cups his hands and blows soap bubbles at me.

They don't pop when they hit me. I stand by the bathtub, covered in bubbles.

I pick up my tire iron and leave.

Dragging the iron against the ground, its scratching a comfort to me. All sweat and shaking. Something terrible is happening to me. And I can't understand it. I go to Q.

Q in the History Center. The History Center is a large brown building, imposing, indiscreet bureaucracy. It used to be a Palace.

I walk through the open gate. Past the rose garden. A sparrow shits on me. I walk on past the sleeping sentinel. Through the imposing double-door.

Q's office is on the 3rd floor. I climb the winding staircase, one hand on the banister in one hand the tire iron, and from every direction sounds swirl around me. Music on the radio. Clacking keyboard keys. Paper whooshing out of printers. Fans, clicking from the ceiling. I reach the 3rd floor. I glide down the hall, feeling like ether, my bones dissolving in me.

A man bumps into me as I'm turning a corner. He is wearing a sharp red suit. His head is bowed towards the ground.

Q, I burst as soon as I'm in her office, spacious, imposing, Q sitting on a swivel chair behind a large oak desk, Q! I slap my hands on the table, drop the tire iron, lean forwards. Q, you've got to help me.

She's reading a memo. She looks up at me. Q's wearing red lipstick, black mascara. Her face doesn't change at the sight of me; she puts down the memo, spreads her lips in a smile.

The men. Q—I swallow the bump in my throat—Q, I know who did the massacre and I know who killed my friends. FF, B, and CoP.

There's a door behind Q, and it opens and a dozen men pour in, wearing face masks and thin red suits. Holding machine guns. Pointing at me. Massacre, Q says, what massacre.

The men in red surround me. I straighten from the desk. Raise my hands above my head. The Clown is there, her associate, upside-down in a corner of the room, making faces at me. Face paint dripping on the floor. Costume unravelling. Q leans back in her chair and surveys me. She looks tired. Irritated. And annoyed.

Q lights a cigarette, blows smoke rings that become nooses around my neck.

The Clown is mouthing at me, the word 'Q.' He's doing this with evil delight. Mouthing 'Q' at me, Q Q Q. The single letter. Q.

You never came here, Q is standing above me, inside the circle of men in red, looming over me, tapping my head with her cigarette, You didn't say this.

The Clown, in his corner, starts juggling small balls painted with the faces of my dead friends. FF. B. CoP. The last sound I hear is a memory, *poet's radio*, transmitting from the neighboring room, orderly and clear, a new machine, the voices sharp and distinct, but I can't decipher it.

The butt of a machine gun cracks against my skull. I wake on the breaking wheel. Again.

Spine cracking with the movement of the wheel. Vertebra by vertebra. Bone by bone. Unzip my DNA.

It's a beautiful double cross. Even I can see that. Even me.

ISSUE SEVENTEEN:
END

My carcass returns to my neighborhood. My house is gone. The ground is smooth where it used to be, like nothing ever stood there. I stand where my living room used to be, then my kitchen, bedroom. The air is heavy with dry heat. The next day there's a mall here, it grows up from the ground, six storeys high where my house used to be.

Overhead, a starling formation. Murmuration. Fleeing the city. And a murder of crows. Blasting through the trees.

Children throw rocks at me. I'm running from children. I see my face in a stream, bloody cheeks, cuts and bruises, gashed lip, hair matted with grease and long to my shoulders. I'm wearing a tattered green shirt. No trousers. The shirt falls over my knees.

Strangers give me charity. I eat in the shrines, feasting on black rice, bread, stale beans.

There are corpses stuffed between the sidewalk cracks.

I visit the circus and they laugh at me. Even the freaks won't take me. A bodybuilder grabs my collar, tosses me onto the street.

I get into street fights. Major and minor scuffles that are broken up by the police, their batons breaking my back. I try to join a beggar mafia but they reject me.

Unfit to beg, I skulk and sleaze. Slouch by the streetlamps, watching cars cut through the streets. Their taillights hurt me.

Scorched by the heat. Distorted by chemicals. Killer smog. Filling my lungs; polluting me.

At night I sleep in doorways, benches, rubbish heaps. There's rubbish everywhere. Accumulating. A cosmic mass.

Sometimes, by accident, a signal catches me. Frazzles a synapse. Leaves me quivering. Just snatches now, snippets. I'm aware of something vast, supreme, of cold beauty— planes above me, forbidden to me.

When it comes it comes in scraps, in mixed missives, as taunt and tease. I have to claw and tear at the air, *unfurl the message that's spelling out on a ticker tape*

G A M E

o v e r

.

.

o v e r

G A M E

Letter by letter. Commit this suicide.

Syphilitic in a city of syphilitics. All more or less syphilitic. Deep in disease. Lungs that defecate. Skin that's paper. Eyes occluded by a black screen.

Every morning I have a banana for breakfast. Given for free. With a penny I buy sugarcane juice. Then the day whittles me away.

One day. In the middle of the road. I see a cockroach crossing. I approach it. Traffic ignores me, it, us. Time stops. The moment swells to infinity, holding just the two of us: me, and the cockroach. The cockroach and I look at each other. It is clicking its antennae. Its wings flutter. I lift my left foot and bring it down in one smooth motion, fluid, unerring, and the cockroach dies in a dramatic scene: crunch of exoskeleton, a smell, grey ooze.

This is perfect contact.

I rip my shirt, tear through the streets. Eviscerated, I'm craving a hit again. Banging on locked doors. Stumbling through streets dissolving in the rain. Then I'm a line of red, staining the sidewalk cracks.

11:11 Press is an American independent literary
publisher based in Minneapolis, MN.
Founded in 2018, 11:11 publishes innovative
literature of all forms and varieties. We believe
in the freedom of artistic expression, the
realization of creative potential, and the
transcendental power of stories.